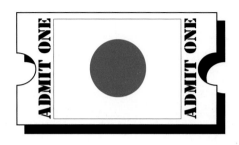

Niihama Castle
on Shikoku

FACES
AND
PLACES

JAPAN

BY ELMA SCHEMENAUER

THE CHILD'S WORLD®

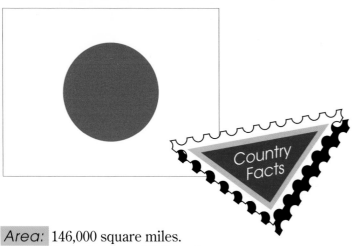

Country Facts

Area: 146,000 square miles.
That is about the size of California.

Population: Over 125 million people.

Capital City: Tokyo.

Other Important Cities: Hiroshima, Kyoto, Osaka, and Nagasaki.

Money: The yen. It is divided into 100 sen.

National Song: "Kimigayo".

National Holiday: Birthday of the Emperor on December 23.

National Flag: A red circle surrounded by white. The red circle represents the beautiful sun that shines on Japan.

Head of the Government: Prime Minister Ryutaro Hashimoto.

Emperor: His Majesty Emperor Akihito.

Library of Congress Cataloging-in-Publication Data
Schemenauer, Elma
Japan / by Elma Schemenauer.
Series: "Faces and Places".
p. cm.
Includes index.
Summary: Examines the geography, history, people,
and customs of the island nation of Japan, which
is only about as big as California but has a population
of over 125 million people.
ISBN 1-56766-371-0 (hard cover, library bound)

1. Japan — Juvenile literature. [1. Japan.] I. Title.
DS806.S363 1998
952 — dc20   96-30663
                                                         CIP
                                                         AC

GRAPHIC DESIGN
Robert A. Honey, Seattle

PHOTO RESEARCH
James R. Rothaus / James R. Rothaus & Associates

ELECTRONIC PRE–PRESS PRODUCTION
Robert E. Bonaker / Graphic Design & Consulting Co.

PHOTOGRAPHY
Cover photo: Child at Japanese Saijo Festival
by Michael S. Yamashita / Corbis

Table
of
Contents

ADMIT ONE   ADMIT ONE

If you could look down on the Earth from high above, you would see large land areas surrounded by water. These land areas are called continents. Some continents are made up of several different countries. Japan is an island country within the largest continent of Asia.

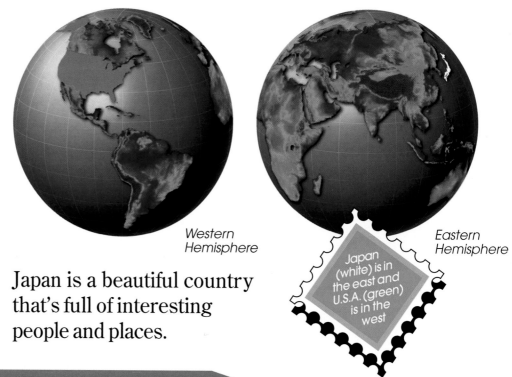

Western Hemisphere

Eastern Hemisphere

Japan (white) is in the east and U.S.A. (green) is in the west

Japan is a beautiful country that's full of interesting people and places.

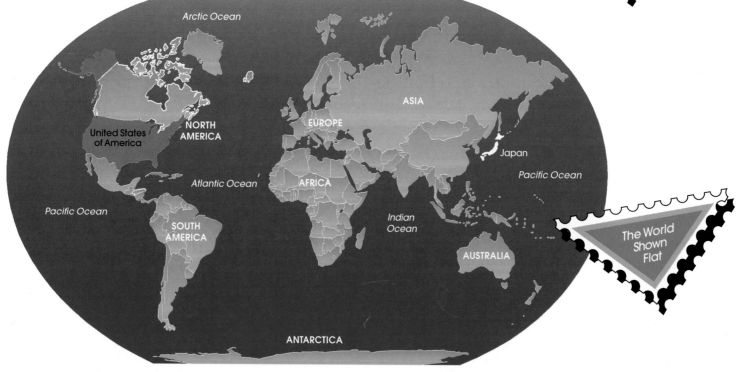

Arctic Ocean

NORTH AMERICA

United States of America

EUROPE

ASIA

Japan

Pacific Ocean

Atlantic Ocean

AFRICA

Pacific Ocean

SOUTH AMERICA

Indian Ocean

AUSTRALIA

The World Shown Flat

ANTARCTICA

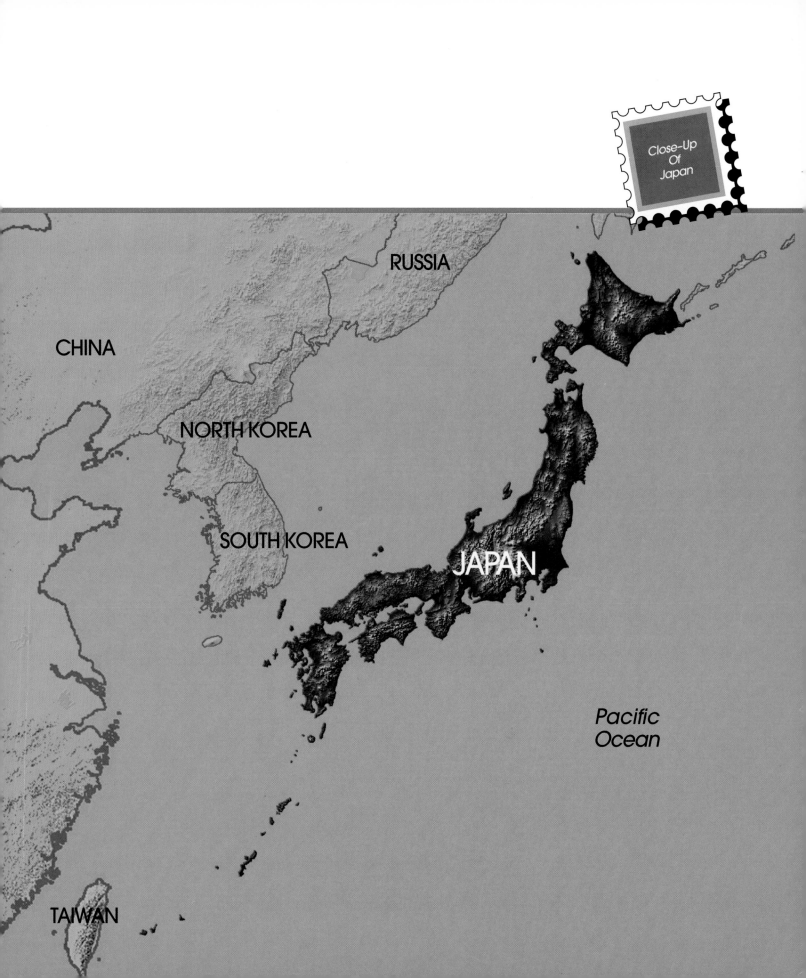

Close-Up
Of
Japan

RUSSIA

CHINA

NORTH KOREA

SOUTH KOREA

JAPAN

TAIWAN

*Pacific
Ocean*

Mount Fuji
On
Honshu
Island

HOKKAIDO

Mount Akan +

HONSHU

Mount Fuji
+

KYUSHU

SHIKOKU

Michael S. Yamashita/Corbis

Volcanic Landscape On Kyushu

Mount Akan On Hokkaido

Most countries are made up of one piece of land. But not Japan! Japan is made up of thousands of islands. The islands were formed long ago when huge volcanoes erupted under the ocean. Hot melted rock called lava spilled out underwater. When the lava cooled, it hardened to form the islands.

Most of Japan's islands are very small. But four of the islands are big enough for people to build cities on. Hokkaido (ho–ky–doh) is a big island in the northern part of Japan. It is covered with mountains and forests. The island of Honshu (hone–shoo) has Japan's highest mountain. It is called Mount Fuji (foo–jee).

It is the highest mountain in Japan. The island of Shikoku (shi–ko–koo) gets lots of rain. Kyushu (kyoo–shoo) has the warmest weather of all Japan's islands.

Inland Sea Off Shikoku

Plants & Animals

ADMIT ONE · ADMIT ONE

Michael S. Yamashita/Corbis

Cherry Blossom Party In Saitama-Ken

Deer At Rest In Hiroshima

Each area of Japan has different plants and animals. Bears and deer live in the forests of Hokkaido. On the island of Honshu, people who go hiking sometimes see eagles. Some areas of Japan have beautiful cherry trees for people to enjoy. In the mountains, people can see red-faced Japanese monkeys. These monkeys are known as macaques (muh–KAKS). Macaques are also called snow monkeys because they live in colder areas.

Michael S. Yamashita/Corbis

HOKKAIDO

HONSHU

Hiroshima

Nagano

SAITAMA-KEN

Michael S. Yamashita/Corbis

Macaque
Monkey
At Spa In
Nagano

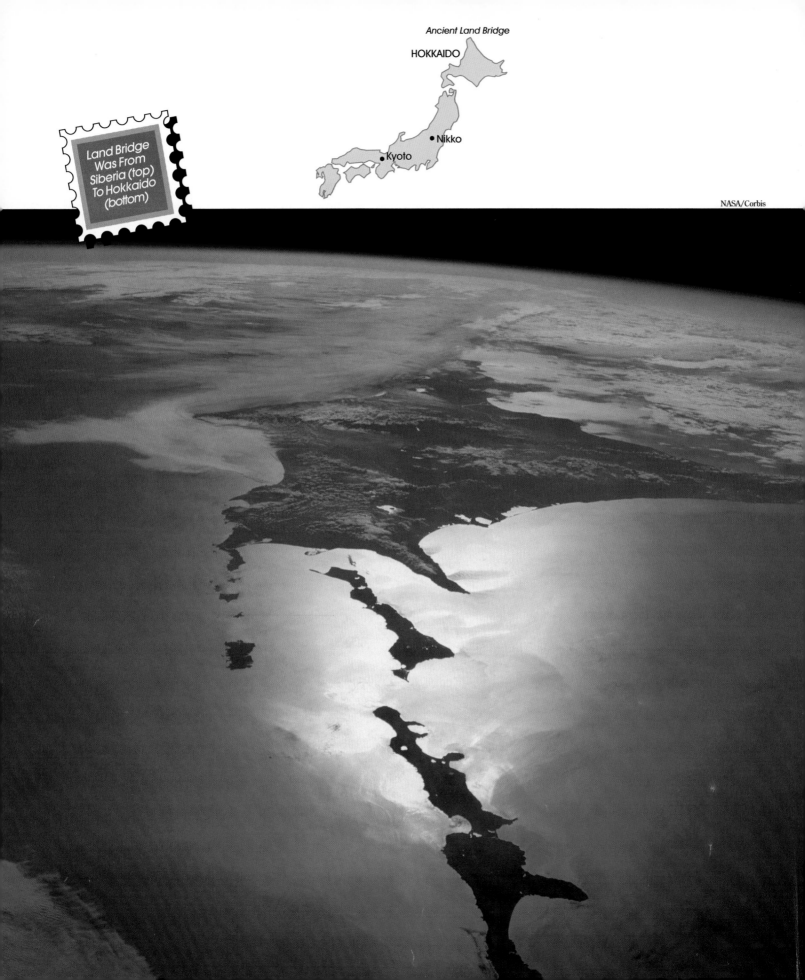

Ancient Land Bridge

HOKKAIDO

• Nikko

• Kyoto

Land Bridge
Was From
Siberia (top)
To Hokkaido
(bottom)

NASA/Corbis

Long Ago

The first people came to Japan about 18,000 years ago. But how did they get there? Long ago, the oceans weren't as deep as they are now. Much of the world's water was frozen into ice. In some places, pieces of land connected the continents together.

These pieces of land are called land bridges. People could walk from one continent to another without having to cross the ocean. They just walked across the ice.

Over time, the earth slowly warmed up. The ice melted and water covered up the bridges. The people who had walked to Japan had to stay there. That is how people came to Japan's islands!

Young Nikko Samurai Dressed Like Ancestor

Dave Bartruff/Corbis

Celebrating Festival Of Ages In Kyoto

Morton Beebe-S.F./Corbis

Japan Today

For a long time, Japan was ruled by emperors. An emperor had a lot of power over the people. Today, Japan's emperor is not very powerful. He does not make rules for the country anymore. Instead, Japan's laws are made by its Parliament. The people in Japan's Parliament talk about how their country is doing. They make laws to keep the Japanese people safe. They also think of ways to make Japan a better place to live.

Woman In Tokyo Voting In 1983

UPI/Corbis-Bettmann

The Purcell Team/Corbis

Parliament Building In Tokyo

The National Archives/Corbis

1940's Picture Of Emperor Hirohito

Michael S. Yamashita/Corbis

Tokyo

Crowded Street In Osaka

Kyoto
Tokyo
Osaka
KYUSHU

Michael S. Yamashita/Corbis

Over 125 million people live in Japan. Most of them live near the coasts of the big islands. If you visited Japan, you would see mostly Japanese faces around you. That's because in Japan, almost everyone is Japanese.

A Kindly Young Face From Kyoto

Dave Bartruff/Corbis

Manners are very important in Japan. Japanese people believe in being polite and treating others with respect. They try to help each other and be good neighbors. Being kind to other people is a very old and important part of Japanese life.

Shopping Time In Tokyo

Kevin Morris/Corbis

Office Workers Share Time On Kyusho

Michael S. Yamashita/Corbis

In Japan, almost everyone lives in cities. The biggest city is Tokyo (tohk–yoh or tohk–ee–oh) on the island of Honshu. Most city families live in apartments. These apartments are very small. That's because Japan's cities are very crowded! In Japan's cities, families must learn ways to save space.

Out in the country, there aren't as many people. Many Japanese country-dwellers live in wooden houses. Usually, these houses are in villages. Some families live on farms. Country people try to help their neighbors and be good friends.

Apartment Style In Urayasu

Kevin Morris/Corbis

Town Layout And Fields In Tokushima

Dave Bartruff/Corbis

Farm House And Beet Field Near Koshimisu

Michael S. Yamashita/Corbis

Koshimizu ●

Urayasu ●

● Tokushima

SHIKOKU

Park Setting On
Shikoku

Michael S. Yamashita/Corbis

Classroom
In
Ajigasawa

Ajigasawa

Tokyo

Kevin Morris/Corbis

Writing
On Stone
From
Kamcido,
Tokyo

Japanese children start school when they are six years old. They learn math and social studies just as you do. Japanese students also learn art, music, and computers. In the upper grades, Japanese children learn how to speak another language—English. Japanese children work very hard. They even go to school on Saturday mornings!

Japanese children learn two alphabets. And they also need to learn about 2,000 letters! It takes that many letters to write in Japanese. Japanese is not an easy language, but it is very interesting. Writing some Japanese words is like drawing pictures. And when you speak some Japanese words, they sound just like what they mean. For example, ki-ki (kee–kee) means "squeaky," and goro-goro means "rumbling."

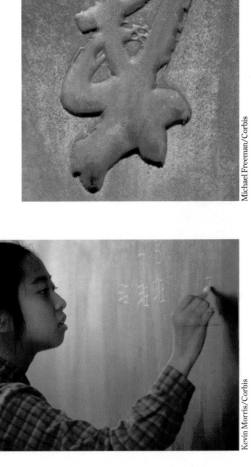

Michael Freeman/Corbis

Student
Workshop At
Christian
Academy
In Tokyo

Kevin Morris/Corbis

Ajigasawa Student
At Blackboard

Kevin Morris/Corbis

Work

In the cities, people work at all kinds of jobs. Some people work in stores or banks. Others work in offices, hotels, and hospitals. Many others work inside huge factories. There they make things such as cameras, computers, and cars.

Farmer Plowing Field On Hokkaido

Michael S. Yamashita/Corbis

Planting A Pearl Bead In An Oyster In Uwajima

Dave Bartruff/Corbis

In the country, Japanese people have other jobs to do. Many people catch fish or collect seaweed to bring to market. Others make boards and paper from trees. Many other people grow crops such as soybeans, rice, tangerines, and apples.

Train Conductor Helps Passenger In Hiroshima

Dean Conger/Corbis

HOKKAIDO

Hiiroshima

KYUSHU Uwajima

Michael S. Yamashita/Corbis

Sushi Bar Workers In Tokyo

Sapporo

Kyoto   Tokyo

Morton Beebe-S.F./Corbis

Food

Japanese people like to eat many different kinds of food. They eat lots of rice and vegetables. They also like to eat spinach, mushrooms, and a kind of radish called a daikon (dy-kohn). Sushi (soo–shee) is a very popular dish. It is made of fish and seaweed. People in Japan eat and cook with special sticks called chopsticks. They hold two chopsticks in one hand and use them to pick up food.

Japanese people love to drink tea. It is served everywhere—in restaurants, in offices, and in homes. Japanese tea is pale green or brown. It is served plain, without sugar, milk, or lemon.

Eating Salmon With Chopsticks In Sapporo

Natalie Fobes/Corbis

Serving Tea In Kyoto

Octopus From The Tsukiji Center In Tokyo

Dave Bartruff/Corbis

Bob Krist/Corbis

Pastimes

Judo, karate, and video games were all invented in Japan! Another popular Japanese sport is sumo (soo–mo) wrestling. People in Japan also play baseball, volleyball, tennis, and golf. Paper folding, called origami (or–i–gah–mee), is a popular hobby.

Many Japanese children enjoy watching TV and playing computer games just like yours. They also read books, magazines, and comic books called manga (man–guh). Some restaurants have stacks of manga for grown-ups to read while they wait for their meals.

Judo Master Honors Student In Sendai

Sumo Wrestlers In Nagasaki

Video Game Center In Osaka

Robert Holmes/Corbis

Visitors Viewing
Cherry Blossoms
In Fukuoka

Sapporo

Matsushima

Tokyo

Kyoto

Fukuoka

Holidays

Japan has many different holidays. November 15 is the 7-5-3 Festival. On that day, Japanese children who are 7, 5, or 3 years old get to put on special robes, called kimonos. Kimonos are worn only on special days. The Cherry Blossom Festival comes when the cherry trees bloom. Families picnic under the cherry trees and write poems about the beautiful blossoms.

The people of Japan mix the old ways with the new. In Japan you might see a hamburger restaurant next to a Japanese tea room. Children may wear blue jeans every day, but for holidays they wear their special kimonos. Japan is a wonderful place to learn about mixing old and new ways together.

Costumes For The Aoi Festival In Kyoto

Eye Ubiquitous/Corbis

Kevin Morris/Corbis

Girl Wearing Kimono In Matsushima

Normal Dress For Tokyo At Night

Michael S. Yamashita/Corbis

スワッナホ

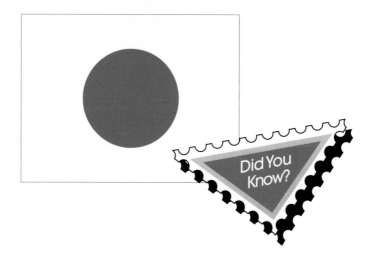

Did You Know?

The Shinkansen (shin-kahn-sen) or "Bullet Train," is a special train in Japan. It is one of the fastest trains in the world—it can go up to 160 miles an hour!

Japan is a country that has a lot of earthquakes. Every year there are about 1,500 small earthquakes, or tremors, all over the country.

Many Japanese people raise bonsai (bon–siy) trees. The trees are very small and are grown in pots. Many people like to trim and shape their bonsai trees so they look different from everyone else's.

How Do You Say?

	JAPAN	HOW TO SAY IT
Hello	konnichiwa	(koh-nee-che-wah)
Goodbye	sayoonara	(sy-oh-nah-ruh)
Please	onegaishimasu	(oh-ne-guy-she-mah-soo)
Thank You	arigato	(ah-ree-gah-toh)
One	ichi	(ee-chee)
Two	nii	(nee)
Three	sun	(sun)
Japan	Nihon	(nee-hohn)

Glossary

chopsticks (CHOP–stiks)
Chopsticks are special sticks that Japanese people use for eating. Two chopsticks are used to pinch food or scoop it up.

continent (KON–tuh–nent)
Continents are huge areas of land. Most of the continents are separated by oceans.

emperor (EM–per–rer)
An emperor is a ruler, like a king. Japan's emperor was once very powerful.

kimono (kih–MO–no)
A kimono is a long robe with wide sleeves. Japanese people wear kimonos on special days.

land bridges (LAND BRI–jez)
Land bridges were narrow pieces of land that connected the continents long ago. People first came to Japan by walking across land bridges.

lava (LAH–vuh)
Lava is hot, melted rock that comes from deep inside the Earth. Japan's islands are made of lava.

macaques (muh–KAKS)
A macaque is a type of monkey that lives in Japan. It is also called a snow monkey.

Parliament (PAR–lu–ment)
A parliament is a group of people that makes laws. Japan has a parliament in Tokyo.